Bettina,

Always Remember -
It is not reaching the
Destination - but how
we make the trip
that matters.

Love,
Anita

P.S. Have a GREAT TRIP!

CIRCLE OF LIFE

FROM DISNEY'S
THE LION KING

CIRCLE OF LIFE

MUSIC BY ELTON JOHN
LYRICS BY TIM RICE

NEW YORK

Bettina,

FROM THE
DAY WE
ARRIVE ON
THE PLANET

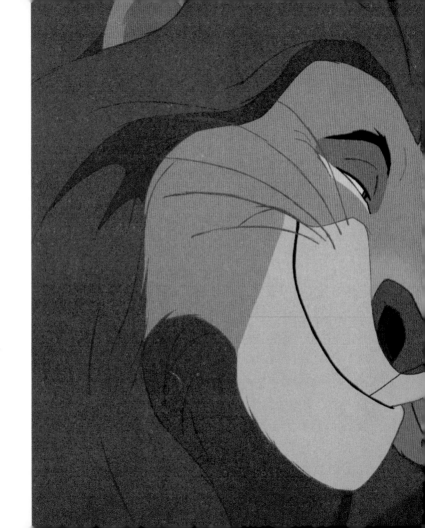

AND
BLINKING
STEP INTO
THE SUN,

THERE'S MORE
TO SEE THAN
CAN EVER BE
SEEN,

MORE TO DO THAN

CAN EVER BE DONE.

THERE'S FAR TOO MUCH
TO TAKE IN HERE,

MORE TO FIND
THAN CAN EVER
BE FOUND,

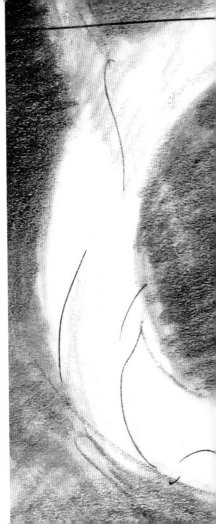

BUT THE SUN
ROLLING HIGH

THROUGH THE
SAPPHIRE SKY

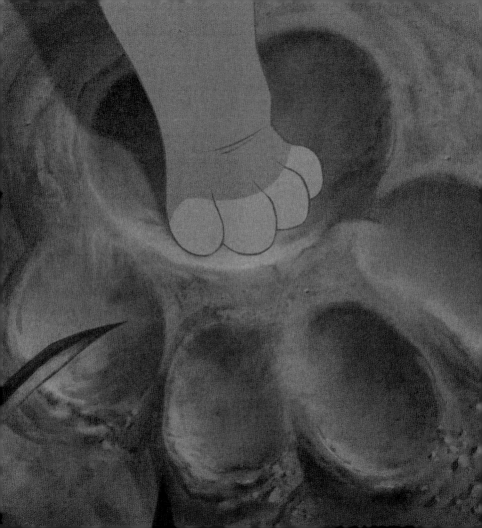

KEEPS GREAT AND SMALL
ON THE ENDLESS ROUND.

IT'S THE CIRCLE
OF LIFE

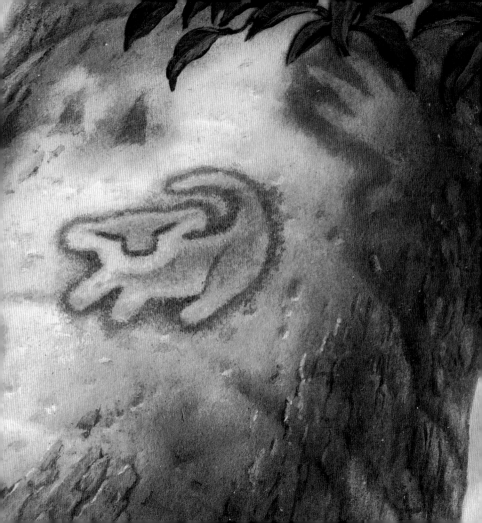

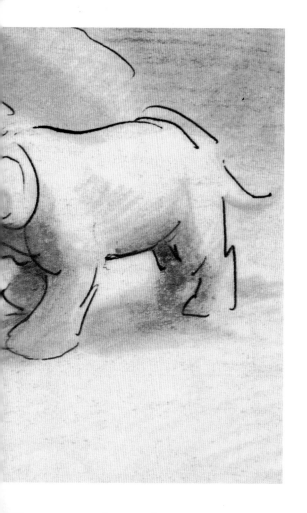

AND IT
MOVES US
ALL,

THROUGH
DESPAIR AND
HOPE,

THROUGH FAITH

AND LOVE,

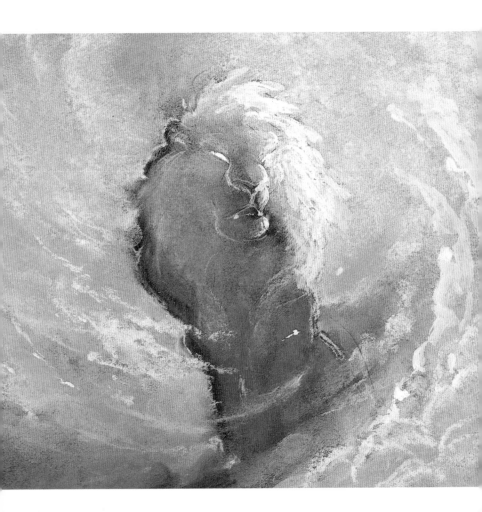

TILL WE FIND
OUR PLACE

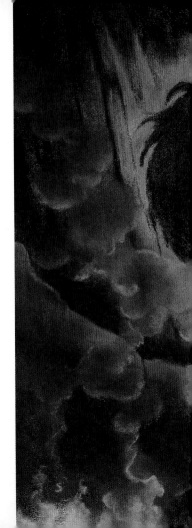

ON THE PATH
UNWINDING

IN THE CIRCLE,
THE CIRCLE OF LIFE,

And it seems like we just
keep going round & round.
Soon it all looks familiar &
we realize we've had this same
relationship, ended it, had it
again, ended it ....
One day soon we'll get it right?

Have Faith &
Don't stop reaching
out for Love &
You will find it!
Love,
Anita

FOR INFORMATION ADDRESS:
HYPERION, 114 FIFTH AVENUE, NEW YORK, NY 10011

PRODUCED BY WELCOME ENTERPRISES, INC.
575 BROADWAY, NEW YORK, NY 10012

ISBN 0-7868-6148-7

FIRST EDITION

2 4 6 8 10 9 7 5 3 1

PRINTED IN JAPAN
BY TOPPAN PRINTING CO., INC.